BOT!

James Yang

VIKING

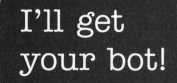

My broom
may reach
that bot!

Honk! This trombone will trap that bot!

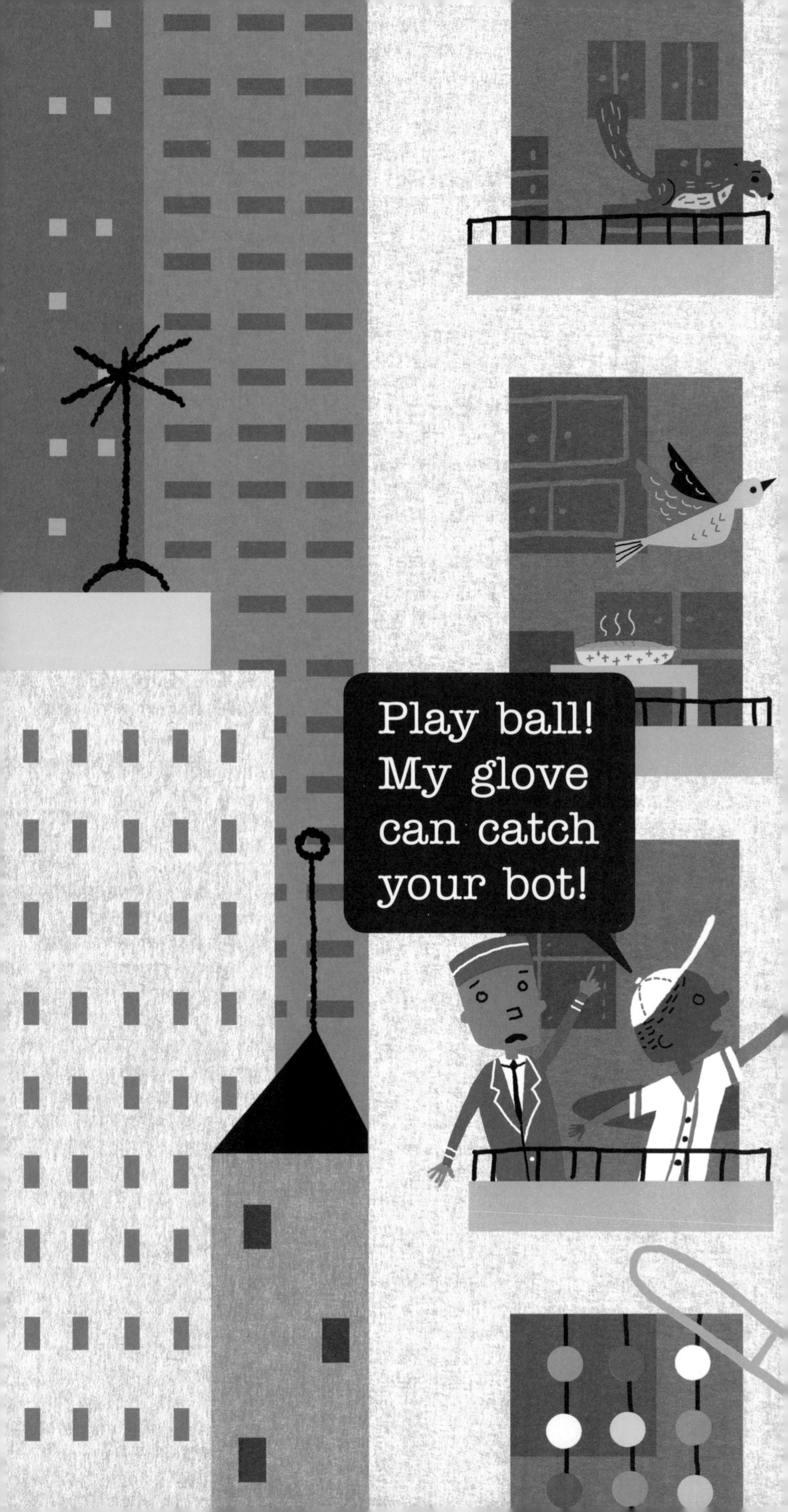
Play ball! My glove can catch your bot!

Giraffes are good at getting bots.

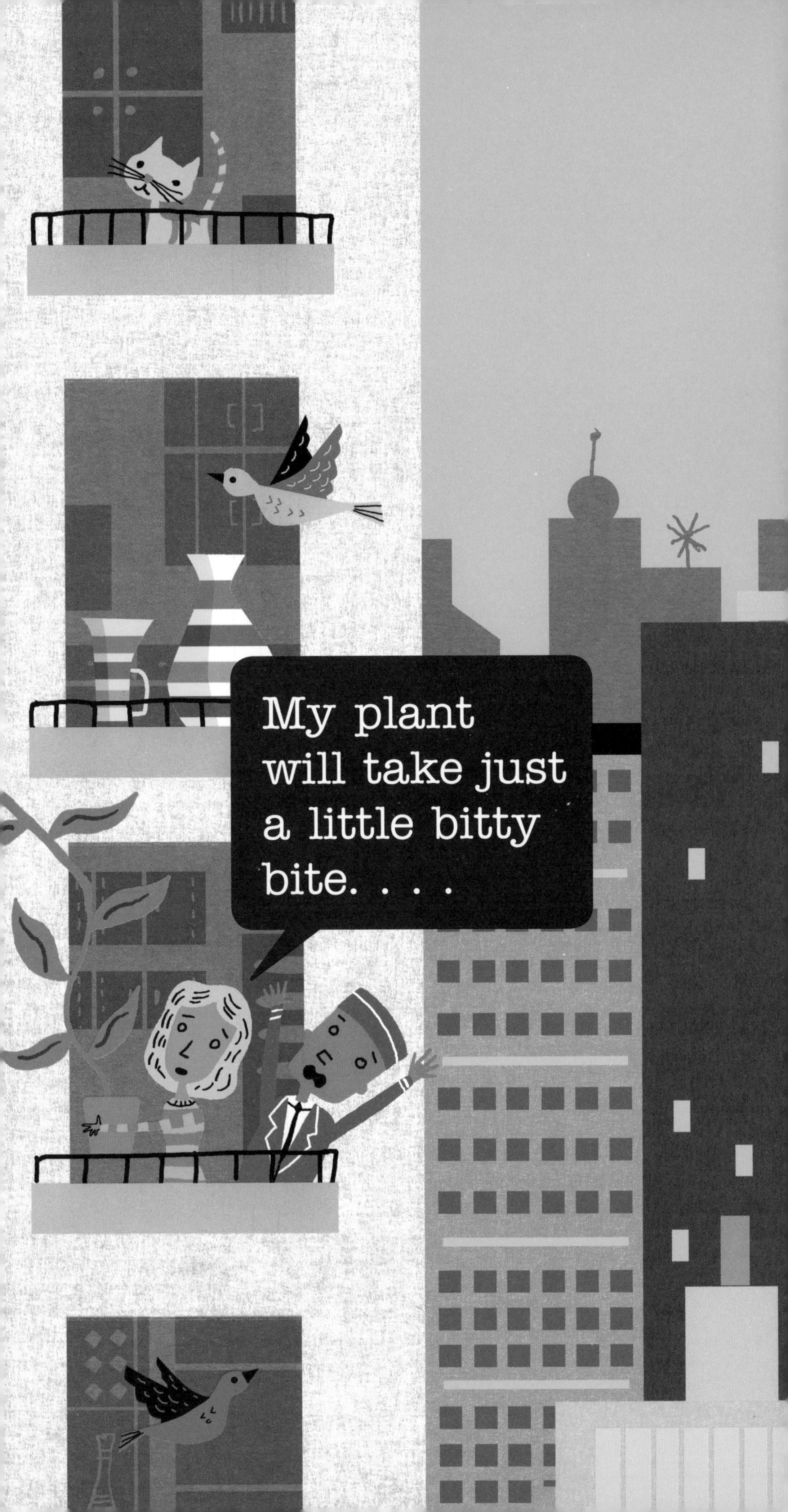
My plant will take just a little bitty bite. . . .

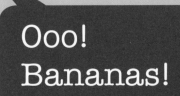

Dedicated to Abby Yang,
who always helps me find things
in tall buildings.

VIKING
Penguin Young Readers
375 Hudson Street
New York, New York 10014

First published in the United States of America by Viking,
an imprint of Penguin Random House LLC, 2019

Visit us online at penguinrandomhouse.com

LIBRARY OF CONGRESS CATALOGING-IN-PUBLICATION DATA IS AVAILABLE.
ISBN 9780425288818

Manufactured in China
Book design by Jim Hoover   Set in ITC American Typewriter

10   9   8   7   6   5   4   3   2   1